Wild Goat

BY Caroline Arnold

PHOTOGRAPHS BY

Richard Hewett

MORROW JUNIOR BOOKS

NEW YORK

1 2 3 4 5 6 7 8 9 10

Library of Congress Cataloging-in-Publication Data. Arnold, Caroline. Wild Goat/by Caroline Arnold; photographs by Richard Hewett. p. cm. Summary: Text and photographs describe the appearance, behavior, mating, growth, predators, and heritage of Daisy and Chaim, two playful wild goats at the Los Angeles Zoo. ISBN 0-688-08824-4.—ISBN 0-688-08825-2 (lib. bdg.)
1. Ibex—Juvenile literature. [1. Goats.] I. Hewett, Richard, ill. II. Title.
QL737.U53A76 1990 599.73'58—dc20 89-38958 CIP AC

Acknowledgments

This book could not have been written without the assistance of the Los Angeles Zoo, and we want to thank everyone there who helped us. In particular we want to express our appreciation to June Bottcher, for helping to make all the necessary arrangements, and to Kim Brinkley, the Nubian ibex keeper (pictured above with Rebecca). We would also like to recognize the Nubian ibex that have been "adopted" by zoo donors as part of the Greater Los Angeles Zoo Association's Adopt an Animal program. In addition to Daisy and Chaim, who are part of our story, the adopted animals are named Prince Pattiken, Tapshoes, Empress, Jajobo, Knucklehead, Twirls, Lancer, and Jessekins. As always, we also thank our editor, Andrea Curley, for her continued enthusiastic support.

The two baby goats scampered across the rocky wall, their tiny feet clinging tightly to the rough stone surface. Although they were just a few days old, Daisy and Chaim were nearly as agile as they would be as adults. They seemed to have no fear of the high ledges and steep walls that were their home. Like the other wild goats in the herd, their sure feet and good sense of balance enabled them to move easily through their enclosure at the Los Angeles Zoo.

Daisy and Chaim were among three pairs of twins and one set of triplets newly born at the zoo. During their first week, Daisy and Chaim and their mother, Golda, spent most of their time behind the rear wall of the exhibit and out of sight of zoo visitors. However, as they grew bigger and more sure of themselves, they soon began to explore the whole enclosure.

The goats at the zoo are Nubian ibex, a kind of wild goat native to the dry, rocky mountains and valleys of northeast Africa and the Arabian peninsula. Although Nubian ibex were once widespread in those areas, their numbers have been severely reduced both because of hunting and because domestic goats have driven them out of many of their former grazing areas. In Israel, where laws now protect Nubian ibex, the herds have begun to increase. By studying ibex, we can learn more about them and help to ensure their survival.

The Nubian ibex seem comfortable at the zoo. The dry, warm climate of Southern California is like that of the Middle East, and their enclosure was made to be as much like their native habitat as possible. It has ledges and boulders for resting; a deep, empty moat that provides shade and a quiet place for the mother goats and their new babies; a flat, open area with a pond for drinking; and an inside area for shelter from rain. Each day the keeper cleans the exhibit and puts out fresh food and water.

In addition to the new baby ibex at the zoo, there were four adult females, one adult male, and a year-old female. Each of the animals was marked with a series of notches on its ears. Although it is often possible to recognize individuals by their size, color, or horn shape, these notches help the keepers to identify each goat more easily, even at a distance. Sometimes the keepers name the goats as well. They usually choose names that reflect the ibex's Middle Eastern heritage. For instance, the adult male at the zoo is called Sadat after Anwar Sadat, a former leader of Egypt; and Daisy and Chaim's mother is called Golda after Golda Meir, a former premier of Israel.

Daisy and Chaim got their names when they were adopted by zoo donors. Like many other zoos, the Los Angeles Zoo allows people to give money and "adopt" one of the animals. The adopted animal does not actually belong to the donor. It remains at the zoo and is cared for by the keepers. However, each donor receives a certificate of adoption and can choose a name for his or her animal.

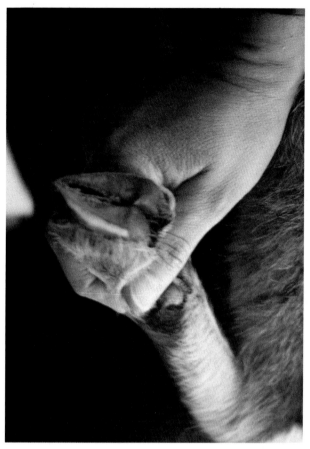

The Nubian ibex is a subspecies of ibex, a kind of wild goat found in high, rocky mountains in Africa, Europe, and Asia. It is an excellent climber, with strong legs and hooves especially adapted for clinging to rough surfaces. The hoof is split, and between the two sides is a soft, fleshy cushion that helps keep the foot from sliding.

Thousands of years ago all ibex probably shared a common ancestor. Subspecies formed as groups of animals separated and moved to new areas, where they changed somewhat in size, color, or behavior as they adapted to different conditions. Although there is some disagreement among scientists about how many kinds of ibex there are, the usual number given is seven.

The Alpine ibex, which nearly became extinct at the turn of the century, is now protected and found throughout the Alps in Europe. The other European subspecies, the Spanish ibex, lives in the Pyrenees mountains of Spain and is very rare. It is distinguished by horns that curve back and out in a partial spiral.

The Siberian ibex has the longest horns of all the ibex, sometimes reaching 60 inches (1.5 meters) or more. It is found in Central Asia, from the Tien Shan and Altai mountains of China to the Himalayas in Kashmir, and is prized for its soft underfur, which is used to make beautiful boots and gloves. In the Caucasus mountains of Eurasia, the two species of ibex are known as the Kuban tur and the Daghestan tur. The Walia ibex, which is similar to the Nubian ibex, but with a darker coat and slightly heavier body, is found only in the Simien mountains of Ethiopia. Like the Spanish ibex, it is an endangered species.

Markhor

The scientific name for the Nubian ibex is *Capra ibex nubiana*. The English word *caper*, which means "to leap or jump about," comes from *capra* and refers to the goat's agility and quick movements. Other members of the *Capra* group include the markhor, which is found in the mountains of Afghanistan and is distinguished by corkscrew-shaped horns; the bezoar, a wild goat of southwestern Asia; and the domestic goat, which is found on farms or kept as a pet. One popular breed of domestic goat, the Nubian, is distinguished by its long, droopy ears. It is not related to the Nubian ibex, though, and should not be confused with it.

Although animals such as the Rocky Mountain goat of North America and the serow, which is found in the mountains of southern Asia, are sometimes called goats, they are not classified with the *Capra* group. They are like goats in some ways, but in other ways are more like antelopes, so they are considered to be goat-antelopes. The tahr, a goatlike animal that lives in the Himalayas, is a link between

Rocky Mountain goats

goats and sheep. Goats, sheep, and antelopes, along with cattle and buffalo, belong to the large animal group called bovines. All of these long-legged animals have horns and are plant eaters. It is differences in bone structure and behavior that distinguish the various groups.

Occasionally domestic animals such as goats are set loose and allowed to fend for themselves. These animals that are returned to the wild are said to be "feral." In the United States, feral goats are found in Texas, California, and Hawaii. Although these goats live like wild animals, they are not the same as true wild goats, such as ibex, which are a different species.

Ibex are moderately large, sturdy animals with thick, strong legs that are somewhat shorter in front than in the back. The Nubian ibex has a light tan-colored coat with a black stripe along the spine, a white chin and underparts, vertical black-and-white stripes on the legs, and a short tail with a black tuft on the end. It is among the smallest of the ibex. A male Nubian ibex is about 4½ feet (137.2 centimeters) long, stands about 33 inches (83.8 centimeters) at the shoulder, and weighs up to 125 pounds (56.8 kilograms). Females are smaller and more slender than males, and usually weigh about half as much.

Up to the age of two years, male and female ibex develop at about the same rate. However, between the ages of two and four, young males begin to differ from females of the same age as their horns grow longer and their bodies continue to increase in size.

Adult males have a scent gland under the tail that gives off a strong odor. Between one and one and one-half years of age, males also begin to grow beards. With domestic goats, males are often referred to as bucks or billies and females as does or nannies. For wild goats, however, these terms are not usually used.

The most obvious distinction between male and female ibex is in their horns, which in the male are much longer and more massive. In both sexes horns are used for fighting. Each horn grows out of the forehead and curves backward in a large arc ending in a sharp point. The side of each horn is flattened and is marked by a series of knobby ridges.

Nubian ibex: male (right), female (left)

16

Unlike the antlers of deer or moose, which are shed and regrown each year, the ibex's horns grow continuously throughout the life of the animal. By measuring the length of the horn, one can estimate the age of the animal. Each horn has an inside bony core that is surrounded by a horny covering. In female ibex, the horns are slender and relatively short compared to those of males, growing up to 24 inches (61 centimeters) or more. A ten-year-old male has horns that can be 60 inches (1.5 meters) or more and weigh as much as 30 pounds (13.6 kilograms). He develops strong neck and shoulder muscles to support this enormous weight. At the zoo, Sadat's horns were so large he had to tip his head sideways to fit through the door to the inside feeding area.

At birth the horns appear as bumps on the head, but by the time the baby ibex is one month old, they are already 2 inches (5.1 centimeters) long. After one year the male's horns are about 12 inches (30.5 centimeters) and at three years they are about 24 inches (61.5 centimeters) long.

As they grow older, male ibex develop larger horns, longer beards, and heavier bodies. Older males also have darker coloring on the chest. Those males that are the biggest and strongest mate the most often. Although a male ibex is able to mate when he is three years old, most mating is done by males five years old or more. Females are able to mate for the first time when they are a year and a half old, although, in the wild, they often do not mate until their third year.

Except during the mating season, adult male ibex live alone or with an all-male herd. Females, on the other hand, live year round in small groups of other females and their newly born young and yearlings, and with males that have not yet joined a male herd.

The mating season is called the *rut*. In the months before the rut begins, males fight among themselves to establish which animals are the strongest. For Nubian ibex the rut occurs in late September and early October. At that time the male herds split up and each older, dominant male joins a female herd and mates with each female. In the wild, mating usually takes place at night; at the zoo, it often occurs in the day. When mating is finished, the male shows no further interest in the female. In the wild, males usually stay with the female herds for about three months, then leave to re-form their all-male groups. At the zoo, the animals stay together year round.

A female ibex is pregnant for five to six months, and the babies, called *kids,* are usually born in late March or early April. Shortly before giving birth, the female climbs to a secluded place. At the zoo females usually give birth in the moat or behind the exhibit wall. One evening in early April, Golda didn't go indoors to eat. The next morning two baby goats lay by her side.

Nubian ibex nearly always produce twins, although occasionally they have triplets or single births. At birth each young kid weighs about 3.6 pounds (1.6 kilograms) and stands about 15 inches (.38 meters) high at the shoulder. Kids are born with their eyes open and can stand almost immediately. Compared to many other kinds of baby animals that are helpless at birth, baby goats are remarkably well developed. On their first day of life, they can walk and follow their mothers, and by the second day they can run and jump. By the age of two weeks, the baby goats are able to jump more than three times their own height.

During the first few days after birth, a mother ibex stays alone with her kids, away from the other goats in her group. At this time the mother and kids get to know each other. Later, when they have joined the other goats, each mother can recognize her own kids by their distinctive smell. If a mother and kid become separated, they call to each other by making bleating noises similar to the "baa, baa" of sheep.

As in other mammals, Daisy and Chaim's first food was Golda's milk. Either one at a time or together, they nursed from the two teats on her udder. Although they soon began to nibble at solid food, milk was their main nourishment until they were about three months old.

When Daisy and Chaim were about a week old, they joined the other young ibex to form a nursery herd. During the day, the mother ibex took turns watching over the kids while the others left to rest or eat. At night each mother slept next to her own kids. In the wild, the nursery herd stays together through the young goats' first year.

Like other hooved animals, goats are plant eaters, and in the wild, their diet consists of grasses and leaves. At the zoo the ibex eat alfalfa hay and nutritional pellets.

Goats have front teeth only in the lower jaw, and they use them to pull up or bite off plants. Food is then chewed with strong, flat molar teeth in the back of the mouth. An ibex has a total of thirty-two teeth. Like other goats, it has tough skin inside its mouth that enables it to eat plants such as nettles, thistles, and brambles without getting hurt.

Nubian ibex are most active in the early morning and late afternoon, and it is then that they search for food. During the middle of the day, they rest and digest what they have eaten. Like many other hooved animals, goats are ruminants, or cud chewers, and their stomachs are divided into four compartments. When food is first swallowed, it goes into the first two

compartments, where bacteria begin to break down the tough plant fibers. Then the food is coughed up and chewed again. After it is thoroughly chewed, it goes to the second set of stomach compartments, and the digestion process is completed.

In hot weather Nubian ibex sometimes feed at night. Like cats and some other animals that are active at night, ibex's eyes contain a substance called tapetum that reflects light and helps them to see in the dark.

The climate where Nubian ibex live in the wild has some of the hottest temperatures in the world, often reaching more than 100 degrees Fahrenheit (37.8 degrees Celsius) in summer. Nubian ibex are well adapted to this harsh environment. By eating when it is cool, they can rest during the hottest part of the day. When they must be in the sun, their shiny summer coats help reflect much of the sun's heat. Also, the base of each hair is dark and this, along with their black skin, helps prevent them from absorbing the harmful ultraviolet rays that cause sunburn. When it is very hot, ibex also pant, and the evaporation of water from the tongue helps them to keep cool. Although they do not need to drink every day, they always stay within a few days' walk from a water hole. At the zoo the ibex can drink at any time from the pond in their enclosure.

In addition to allowing the ibex to conserve energy by feeding during the cooler parts of the day, cud chewing also permits an animal to eat quickly and then move to a safer place to chew its food. The chief natural predator of Nubian ibex is the leopard, although eagles and other large birds of prey can be a danger to young animals. If a member of the herd spots a predator, it makes a loud whistling snort to warn the other animals. Ibex have good eyesight. Because their eyes are located on either side of the head, they also have a wide view of any possible dangers and can usually spot a threat before it gets too close. Although they can use their horns to defend themselves, ibex most often flee from danger instead. Females and younger ibex can usually move quickly enough to escape predators, but as males grow older and heavier they can no longer move as fast. Most ibex eaten by leopards are the slow-moving, older males. In the wild there are few male ibex older than ten. At the zoo, of course, there is no danger from predators and the ibex can live ten to eighteen years or more.

Daisy and Chaim and the other young ibex at the zoo grew rapidly, and by the time they were a month old, they had more than doubled their weight at birth. Ibex are curious about their environment; and as the kids began to explore their enclosure, they soon discovered that they were not the only kind of animal that lived there. Under the large rocks near the front of the exhibit was a family of rock hyraxes. These furry, brown animals, which look something like woodchucks, often live side by side with ibex in the wild.

The hyraxes at the zoo like to climb on top of the rocks and sit in the late afternoon sun. Sometimes a younger goat gives a hyrax a gentle butt as if wanting to play, but usually the two animals ignore each other.

The hyrax seems to be a strange combination of several animals. Said to be the closest living relative to the elephant, it has hooflike feet, a skeleton similar to that of a rhinoceros, lower teeth like a hippopotamus, leg bones and a brain like an elephant, and a stomach like a horse. Fossils suggest that all of these animals probably had a common ancestor millions of years ago. Today there are many species and subspecies of hyrax which can be found in Africa, on the island of Zanzibar, and on the Arabian peninsula. They usually live in colonies of six to fifty animals from several family groups.

Young hyraxes are born in the spring. When they are old enough to venture out from under their rock home, the parents watch over them carefully. If any of the ibex come close at that time, the hyraxes quickly chase them away, nipping at their heels with sharp teeth.

Like other young animals, the ibex kids seemed to enjoy playing with each other. Together they explored all the nooks and crannies of their home as they climbed among the rocks. Each day their muscles grew stronger as they ran and chased each other across the enclosure and up and down the steep walls.

Often the kids' play developed into pushing-and-shoving matches. As early as two weeks of age they began to butt each other with their foreheads, even before their horns had started to grow. Sometimes they even tried to jump up and butt each other, just as the older goats did. Later on, these playful contests would develop into bigger battles to determine who was the leader of the group.

Within both the male and female groups of ibex there is a social structure in which the strongest and largest animals dominate the younger, weaker ones. The dominant animals get first choice of food and resting places. The position of leader is determined by fights in which the animals butt heads and horns, each one trying to force the other to retreat.

Most fights take place between animals of the same age and sex. A female fights to become the leader within her social group. Males fight for leadership within their groups and for the privilege of mating with females. A dominant male usually keeps his position for two or three years before he is replaced.

In a full-fledged battle, the two ibex rear up on their hind legs and throw their full body weight at each other. In an adult ibex, the force of such a blow is sometimes enough to snap a horn.

At the zoo Sadat was the only adult male, so he did not need to fight to keep his position. And because he was the biggest and had longer horns than any animal in the group, the other ibex always let him go first. Golda, the largest and most dominant female in the group, was periodically challenged by the other females. In general, ibex with the longest horns are the leaders in their herds.

Once the social order of an ibex group has been established, usually there is little fighting. When two ani-

mals meet, the dominant animal usually lowers its head and presents its horns to indicate that it is the leader and that the other animal should let it go first. This sometimes leads to butting, but not a serious fight. It is easier to attack from above, and the dominant animal always tries to get above the other ibex, either by climbing on a rock or circling onto a rising slope. Nubian ibex are not territorial and do not defend the area in which they live against other ibex.

Although horns are used chiefly for fighting and as a symbol of social position, they are also handy as back scratchers. The ibex simply has to lean back and move its head to scratch. Ibex also use their teeth and feet for scratching and to keep themselves clean. A mother ibex grooms her babies until they are a year old.

During the molting season, small tufts of hair sometimes catch on the ends of the horns. Ibex molt each spring, shedding the longer hairs of their warmer winter coats. Although days are usually warm where ibex live, winter nights can be chilly, especially at high elevations.

Ibex do live in different places depending on the season, usually spending the summer months close to water holes and the wetter winter months feeding farther away. Each herd has its own feeding, rutting, and birthing areas, and uses the same ones year after year.

Humans have been associated with ibex for a long time. Ibex horns have been prized as trophies by hunters. In the Middle Ages rings made from ibex horns were considered to be magic and were worn to prevent disease. People also believed that ibex blood was a cure for warts, and hairballs found in the stomachs of ibex were used to treat cancer.

Ibex have also been used as a source of meat and milk. Archaeologists have found bones of ibex that were killed by people in pre–Stone Age times as well as pictures of ibex drawn on rock walls.Goats were among the first wild animals to be tamed by people. Scientists believe that goats were probably first domesticated in the area that is now Israel. Over thousands of years, goats that were born and raised in captivity and used as farm animals became a separate subspecies.

Wild goats such as ibex that are brought up with people adapt easily to captivity. At the zoo it is sometimes necessary for a Nubian ibex kid to be raised in the zoo nursery. Then, when the young goat is old enough to take care of itself, it is returned to the ibex enclosure to live with the other animals. This is what happened with a young Nubian ibex named Rebecca. Because she was brought up by people, she has remained friendly with the keepers and likes a pat on the head or a handful of food each time a keeper comes into the enclosure.

In the wild, ibex kids remain close to their mothers until they are nearly a year old. When their mother is ready to give birth again, she leaves them to find a quiet place for her new babies, and they join the other year-old goats in the herd. By this time they will be able to take care of themselves. At the zoo Daisy and Chaim will stay with Golda until they are ten or eleven months old. Then they and the other kids will go to another zoo. This will make the zoo enclosure in Los Angeles less crowded when the new babies are born. At their new home they will be able to breed with other ibex to which they are not so closely related. This helps produce stronger, healthier animals.

Ibex are fascinating animals with an ancient history. Most people will never have the chance to see them in the wild. However, they breed well in captivity and can be seen in many zoos. By observing them close up, we can get to know them better and learn more about these surefooted, playful wild goats.

Index